NO MORE ANIMALS!

by Lucia Monfried
and Betsy James

Dutton Children's Books

NEW YORK

Text copyright © 1995 by Lucia Monfried
Illustrations copyright © 1995 by Betsy James

Library of Congress Cataloging-in-Publication Data

Monfried, Lucia.
No more animals! / [written] by Lucia Monfried and
[illustrated by] Betsy James.—1st ed.
p. cm.—(Speedsters)
Summary: Charlie has some unusual pets, but when he adds
a skink to his collection, his mother thinks he's gone too far.
ISBN 0-525-45390-3
[1. Pets—Fiction. 2. Skinks—Fiction.] I. James, Betsy, ill.
II. Title. III. Series.
PZ7.M743No 1995 94-47572
[Fic]—dc20 CIP AC

Published in the United States by Dutton Children's Books,
a division of Penguin Books USA Inc.
375 Hudson Street, New York, New York 10014

Printed in U.S.A.
First Edition
10 9 8 7 6 5 4 3 2 1

For Taya,

with our cats and birds

L.M.

For Mimi,

remembering all those frogs

B.J.

No More Animals!

I have a lot of animals.
One mouse.

One garter snake.

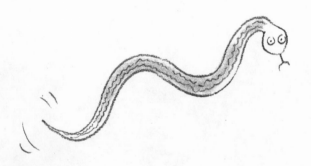

One cicada.

One cat.

One sister—oops! Sorry.

I say, "The more, the merrier." But that's
not what Mom says.

She says, "NO MORE ANIMALS!"

Sometimes she says it like this:

And sometimes she says it like this:

Mom doesn't like animals much. She would
be happy with just one cat.

But here's my problem: Everyone knows I
love animals. So they're always bringing me
more. And I have a hard time saying no.
That's how I got the mouse,

the garter snake,

and the cicada.

And that's how I got the skink.

It was Animal Exercise Time. That's at 3:00 every afternoon when I come home from school.

All my animals are allowed out of their cages in my room. But I have to keep the door closed. And everyone has to get along.

Everyone *does* get along except the cat. The cat is scared of the mouse.

My friend Billy knocked on my window.
I told him to climb in and shut the window
because it was Animal Exercise Time. He was
holding something in his hands.

"Billy, he's great," I said. "But you know my mother said no more animals. I'm scared she's going to make me get rid of the ones I already have."

I know, but one more can't hurt.

And I don't have anyplace to keep him myself.

So I said I'd keep him.

"Yay!" said Billy. "I knew you'd like him."

"Do you have a terrarium to put him in?" asked Billy.

The snake was already using the terrarium. So I decided I would put the skink in the bathtub for now. And I would worry about Mom later.

The Great Escape

Billy and I ran down the hall and put the skink in the tub. Our bathtub is extra deep, with slippery sides. It's a great place to keep a skink.

This is what we found out from the book:

Skinks can run very fast.

A skink's tail is very delicate. In fact, it can come off. This is in case anything tries to catch it.

The skink then grows a new tail. But the new tail is not as good as the old one.

Skinks live in fields and on hills, but they can live in a terrarium or a box with a screen for a lid. They need a dish of water to drink. They eat crickets and mealworms, which you can buy at a pet store.

A skink must be handled gently. If it is scared, its tail can come off.

Skinks don't like to be TOO HOT.

Like a snake, a skink is a cold-blooded reptile. If it gets too hot, it might die.

Skinks don't like to be too cold, either. But when it's cool, a skink gets slow and sleepy.

That's because its blood cools down.

I was so busy reading about skinks that I never heard Mom coming down the hall. Billy heard her, though.

17

And that started her going.

"A skink! That's a new one. And I said no more animals. Take the skink out of the sink," she said.

"You mean the tub," I said.

"I mean I told you: No more animals," she said.

"Not even a cold-blooded reptile?"

"No, I don't want a cold-blooded reptile in my bathtub."

"But it's for a scientific study."

Sometimes if I say I'm doing a scientific study, she lets me do what I want. But not today.

18

She told me to take the skink back to where it came from.

But that was the trouble. I didn't know *where* it came from. Billy had gotten it. Besides, I could never find one as great as this one.

Look at his tongue, Mom. Isn't it CUTE?

She didn't think it was cute. She told me
to find a box for the skink and take it back
to Billy.

Then she sighed. "It's so hot today. I'm
going to sit in the garden and sip iced tea. I
don't want any trouble, Charlie. Especially
animal trouble. Really (*sigh*), I think it would
be a good idea if you let them all go."

"Aw, Mom," I groaned.

But I did go and find a box for the skink.

I was going to remind Mom that I took good care of my animals, but she had already gone back outside.

Just in time! Because as soon as I looked up, I knew I was in animal trouble. BIG animal trouble.

Big Trouble

How did I know?
I saw the cat run by.

Our cat never runs—except when he's scared.
Then I saw the mouse run by.

She was running after the cat. She was *scaring* the cat.

I ran down the hall to my room.

The mouse cage was empty.

The terrarium was empty.

The cicada's jar was empty.

My room was empty!

All the animals had left. I had been so excited about the skink that I had left the door to my room wide open during Exercise Time.

I yelled so loud I was sure Mom would come running.

Then I had another terrible thought. I had probably scared the tail right off my skink. I opened the box to look.

Out zipped the skink—with his tail still on. He took off down the hall like a bullet. Now *every* animal was loose!

How to Catch a Mouse

I knew I had to get the skink and all my
animals back into their cages before Mom
found out. There was no time to lose.

I had no idea where the skink had gone.
But I had seen the mouse heading for the
living room, so I started there.

And there she was. Boy, was I happy! Now all I had to do was catch her. I tried to get the cat to help.

He was useless. He hid under a jacket on a chair.

So I knew it was up to me to catch that mouse.

WHUMP!

GRAB ZIP!

I yanked off my baseball cap.

I grabbed the cage from my bedroom and stuffed the mouse into it.

Then I headed back to where I had seen the skink.

How to Catch a Skink

I figured since the skink was new to our house, he wouldn't know his way around very well.

What he did know was how to run real fast.

I needed to get that skink to a cooler place to slow him down. That's what the book said. Finally I sort of...

herded him...

onto the dishtowel...

and cornered him.

It wasn't even hard.

33

What's cool on a hot day?

I had a really good idea. I got a gallon of ice cream out of the freezer and set it on the counter.

Then I put the skink in a plastic box, with the lid open just a crack for air.

Then I put the plastic box on top of the ice cream.

Chill!

This way, the skink would get cool but not cold.

Things were going great. My mouse was in her cage, and the skink was safe. He still had his tail, and he was chilling out. And Mom didn't know a thing.

How to Catch a Snake

I looked for the snake all over the place.
I mean I looked *everywhere*.

I tried all the places I thought a snake
might like to crawl into.

Then I thought of my sister's room. Mom
says Brenda's room is a jungle. Snakes like
jungles.

My sister was playing dress-up.

I promised Brenda that if she told me
where the snake was I would let her hold
my skink. But only if she was careful with
the tail.

She was wearing my garter snake around
her neck as a necklace.

I wish I had a normal sister who was scared
of snakes.

I also wish I had a normal cat who wasn't afraid of mice.

But at least I had the snake. Whew! I put him in the vase and placed the mouse cage on top. I'd put the snake back in the terrarium later. Right now I had other wildlife to find.

The skink is in the kitchen. You can hold him if he's chilled.

Chilled?

Suddenly I got worried. I could hear somebody in the kitchen.

THUMP!
BUMP!
RUSTLE!

I didn't think Mom would be happy about ice cream out on the counter. And I had one more animal to find.

I was right about Mom. I always am.

I tried to explain that I was doing a
scientific study. But Mom didn't listen.

Mom was mad. She told me to put the ice
cream back while she went outside to water
the roses.

When Mom left, Brenda beat me to the counter and grabbed the box.

But I was too late.

I guess the skink wasn't cold yet. He was still really fast.

Mom heard us yelling. She came inside to find out WHAT WAS GOING ON?

Mom left. Brenda and I started the skink
hunt.

We chased that skink all over the house—
behind the couch...

under the chair...

50

around the vase...

through the bathroom...

I think we wore him out. Because finally,
behind the living-room curtain...

I got him.

How to Catch a Cicada

I gave the skink to Brenda...

because just at that moment, the phone in the hall began to ring. Boy, was I in luck!

The cicada always sings when the phone rings. He thinks the phone is another cicada.

(I told you nobody in our house is normal.)

The phone rang and rang.

I let it ring.

And ring. And ring.

CHARLIE!
BRENDA!
GET THE PHONE!

54

Sure enough, the cicada started to sing—
if you can call it singing. I followed the sound.
He had hopped into Brenda's room and was
sitting on the flowered bedspread, screeching
away.

I got the plastic box and gently scooped the
cicada into it.

We never did find out who called.

Is Everybody Happy?

All my animals were safe again.
The cicada was in the plastic box.

Brenda had the skink.

The snake was in the vase.

The mouse was in her cage on top of the vase.

The cat was asleep under the jacket on the chair. You *can't* lose him.

I thought Mom would be impressed.

OK, MOM!

You can come in now!

It's safe!

But she wasn't.

Charlie, you are going to take those creatures back to your room **RIGHT NOW.**

I did what she asked.

I wanted Brenda to help. But she wouldn't
let go of the skink.

He
LIKES
me!

I even put the ice cream back in the freezer.
It was pretty soupy.

Mom felt much better. "I've been thinking, Charlie," she said. "I was a little hard on you. You're usually so responsible with your animals. Now about the skink..."

"How about this?" said Mom. "That skink has had a hard day. Why don't you keep him till suppertime? Then call Billy. Find out where the skink came from and take him back. He can go home to his family and rest."

Mom made him a house from an old plastic box. She even helped us poke holes for air and put in some grass and water.

We set the box on the windowsill.

"And now," said Mom, "if everybody's happy, I need to sit and rest. But Charlie— NO MORE ANIMALS! You know I'd be happy with just one cat."